God's Love in my Heart

Little Ted's Love Lesson

God's Wonderful World

THIS BOOK BELONGS TO

....

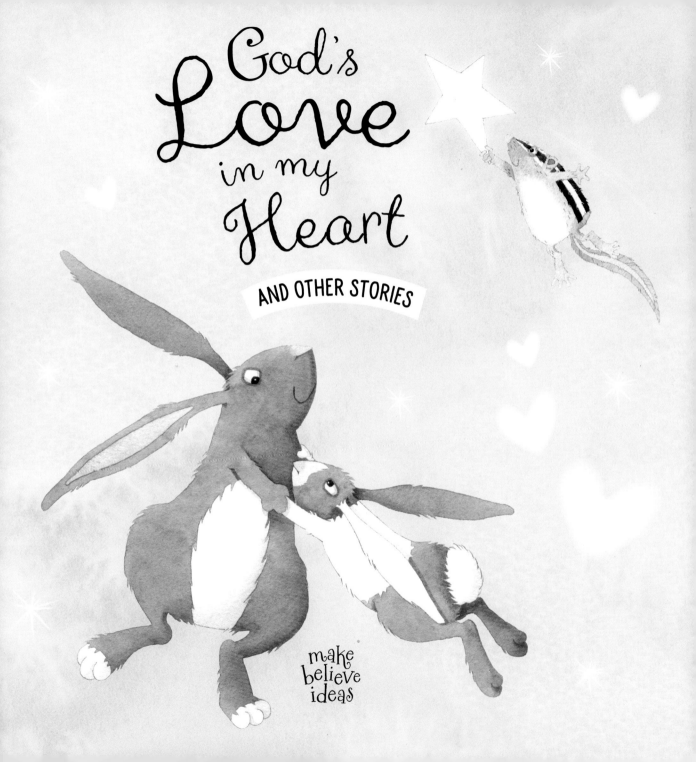

♥ CONTENTS ♥

God's Love in my Heart

Tim Bugbird • Nadine Wickenden

9

Big and Boo were resting
after bouncing in the forest all day.
They were a long way from home,
and Boo was very tired.

"I don't think I can make it all the way back to the burrow," said Boo. "My paws are just too sore!"

Big smiled and took Boo's hand.

"Well, I know you can," said Big.

"And do you know why?"

"Because God's love in our hearts makes us strong!"

As they walked, Big began to explain . . .

13

God's love is so sweet.
It can scent every flower.

God's **love**

is so **calm**.

It turns **storms**

into showers.

God's love
is so big.
It soars up
past the trees.

It's **mighty** enough

to rush **streams**

towards the **seas.**

21

God's love is so bright.
It can light up the night . . .

and softly cap mountains

with blankets of white.

25

God's love is so happy.
Grey skies turn to blues.
His love paints each rainbow with colourful hues.

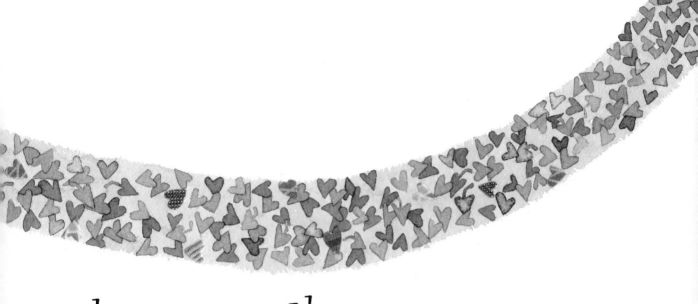

His *love* is so endless.

It goes on and on

and carpets your pathway,

no matter how long.

God's love is so big. It's amazing. It's huge!
Wait, can you feel it? It lives inside you!

With God's love
in our hearts, we can be really strong
and do kind and thoughtful things all the day long!

Before they knew it, Big and Boo were home, snuggled up in their cosy burrow.

"Isn't God's love amazing?" Big whispered to Boo.

But Boo was sound asleep, dreaming of God's big love.

33

THE END

Little Ted's Love Lesson

Rosie Greening · Nadine Wickenden

In a **beautiful** wood,

Little Ted liked to **play**,

and he knew in his heart

Jesus **loved** him each day.

But Ted's **friends** weren't sure

if the Lord loved them too,

and Ted **longed** to show

all his friends it was **true**.

Ted said one evening,
"I wish they could see
that Jesus loves them
in the way He loves me."

38

"I'll build something special,"

decided the bear,

"to show all my friends

just how much Jesus cares."

He cried, "I'll make something as **big** as His LOVE:

a **huge** heart of flowers

that **towers**

above!"

He **gathered**
some tree bark
and **branch bundles** too,

then stuck them together

with **honeycomb** glue.

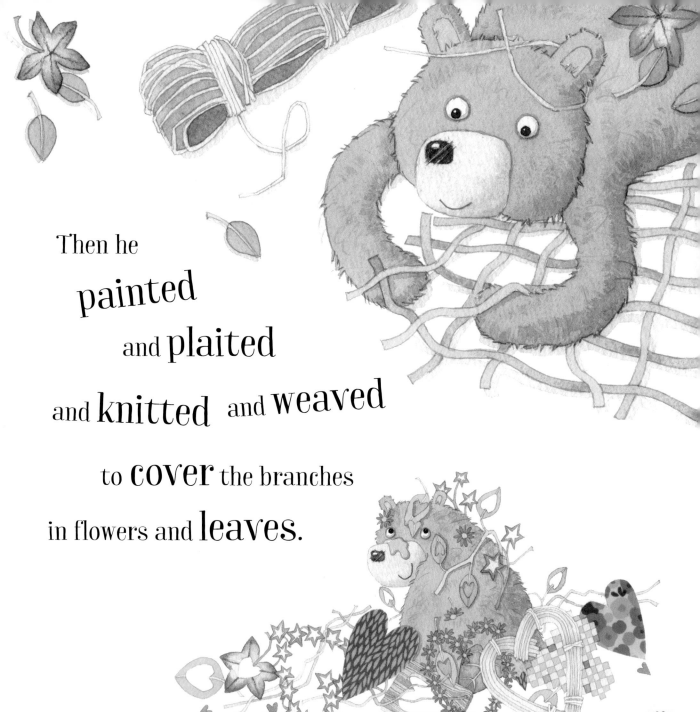

Then he
painted
and **plaited**
and **knitted** and **weaved**

to **cover** the branches
in flowers and **leaves.**

43

44

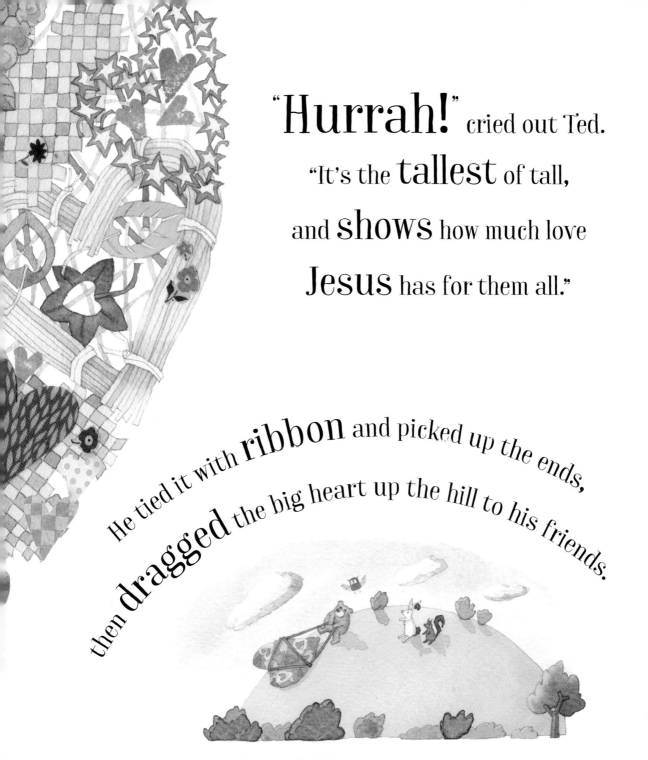

"Hurrah!" cried out Ted.
"It's the **tallest** of tall,
and **shows** how much love
Jesus has for them all."

He tied it with **ribbon** and picked up the ends,
then **dragged** the big heart up the hill to his friends.

"I've made you a gift," cried the sweet little bear. "This heart is to show you how much Jesus cares."

"WOW!" said his friends, as they rushed up to stare.

"We didn't know Christ had so much love to share."

Owl said, "I'll carry it up to my **tree,**
as a lovely **reminder** that Jesus loves **me.**"

He **pulled**
and he **pecked**
and he **tugged**
at the **gift,**

but the **flowery heart**
was **too heavy** to lift!

So Rabbit piped up,

"Let's give MY home a try!"

And the friends dragged the heart

to her burrow nearby.

But the heart was so big,

and the burrow so small,

that the friends couldn't

push the heart

down there at all.

Then **shy** little Squirrel squeaked, "What about me? Perhaps it will **fit** in my **hole** in the tree."

But the hollow had **hundreds**
of acorns inside –

there just **wasn't room**

for a heart of that **size!**

Poor Ted cried, "It's hopeless!
The heart is too tall.
How will you remember
that Christ loves you all?"
But Owl said, "Don't worry –
it's still great to see
just how BIG and amazing
the Lord's love can be."

55

But then the heart **wobbled** and started to **sway**, as a **huge** gust of wind blew the whole thing away.

"**Oh, no!**" cried out Ted,

and he started to dash

as they **heard** in the **distance** ...

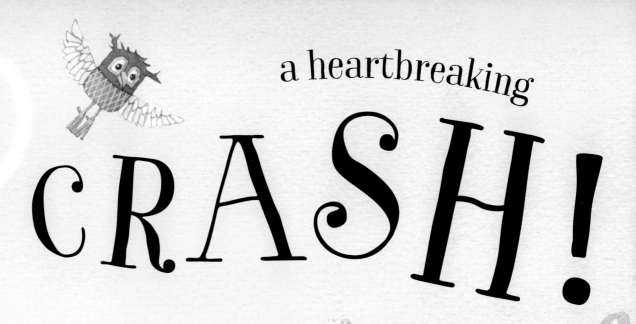

a heartbreaking

CRASH!

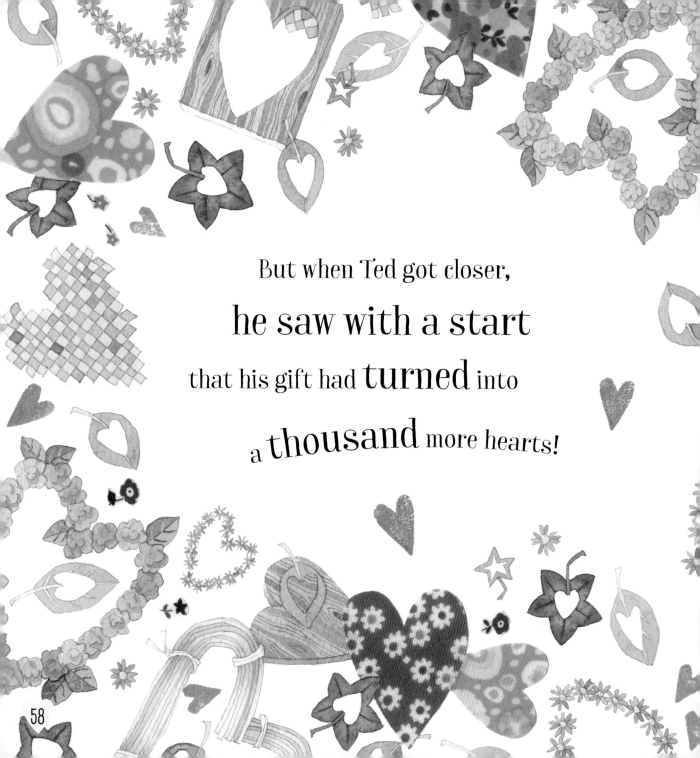

But when Ted got closer,

he saw with a start

that his gift had **turned** into

a **thousand** more hearts!

"Perfect!" cried Ted.

"They're lovely and small.

Now you'll remember

His love after all!"

His friends hung the **hearts**

in a special display,

to **remind** them that God

always loved them each day.

Little Ted learnt that Jesus
is beyond compare.
His love's greater than great,
for the whole world to share.

61

THE END

God's Wonderful World

Alexandra Robinson · Natalie Wallace

As the **sun** begins to **rise** and the
curtain of **night** disappears,
God's **world** prepares for a brand-new **day**.

Butterflies **flitter-flutter** around, a woodpecker **knock-knocks** on a tree and the **flowers** stretch out their **pretty** petals.

Inside a cosy burrow, a young chipmunk is waking up. "I can't wait for my first day outside the burrow!" cries Little Zig.

"Oh, Little Zig," says Big, smiling warmly. "God gave us so many places to explore in His wonderful world."

"Really?" says Little Zig, excitement shining in his eyes.

"Yes, Little Zig, let's go and see some of God's creations," says Big.

And with that, they set off on an adventure . . .

67

God made the sun
that shines so bright,

to warm our hearts and give us light.

He chose a light blue to fill up the sky -

70

a space to give creatures the
freedom to fly.

On land, He planted different seeds to give us all the plants we need.

And from those **seeds** grew many $trees$ –

to make new homes
for birds and bees.

God made the **nuts**

fall at our **feet**

to give us **tasty**

food to **eat.**

God gave us water everywhere,
in lakes and streams
and in the air!

God's birds sing songs that float up high

82

and **form** the sweetest lullaby.

God gave the **spiders** special **thread** to weave **silk** webs in **flowerbeds**.

At **night,** when we all **close** our **eyes,**

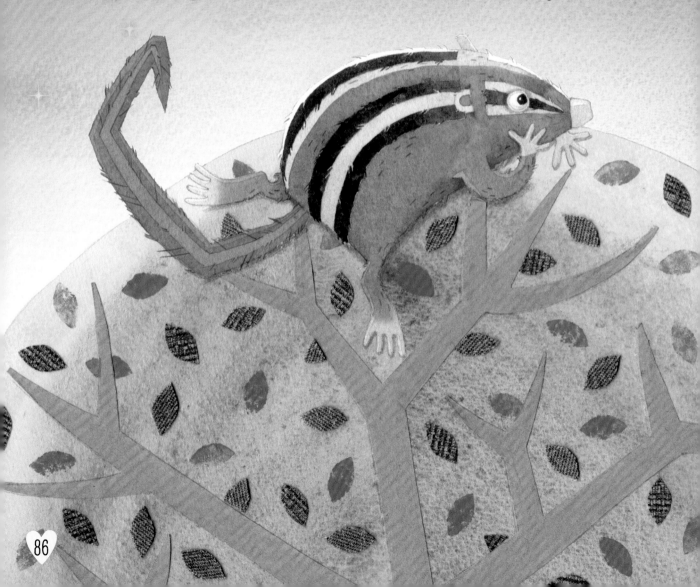

God brings us dreams
until sunrise.

The chipmunks returned to their burrow
and Little Zig fell fast asleep.

Big smiled and kissed him on the forehead.
"What a busy day we've had exploring
God's world," he whispered.

"Goodnight, Little Zig,
and God bless you."

THE END

God's Love in my Heart

Little Ted's Love Lesson

God's Wonderful World